just
in
case
you
want
to
fly

julie fogliano

christian
robinson

WALKER BOOKS
AND SUBSIDIARIES
LONDON · BOSTON · SYDNEY · AUCKLAND

First published in the UK 2020 by Walker Books Ltd
87 Vauxhall Walk, London SE11 5HJ

Published by arrangement with Holiday House Publishing, Inc.

2 4 6 8 10 9 7 5 3 1

Text © 2019 Julie Fogliano
Illustrations © 2019 Christian Robinson

Printed in China

This book has been typeset in Futura Std Heavy

British Library Cataloguing in Publication Data:
a catalogue record for this book is available from the British Library

ISBN 978-1-4063-9167-1

www.walker.co.uk

for clio rose,

who fills my bag with just-in-cases

and for all the little birds with big places to go – j.f.

for ben butcher – c.r.

just in case you want to fly
here's some wind

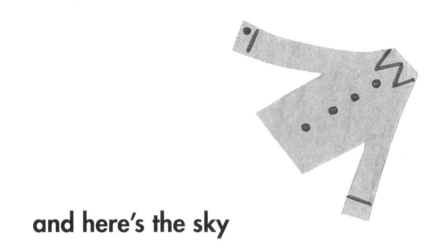

and here's the sky

here's a feather
here's up high

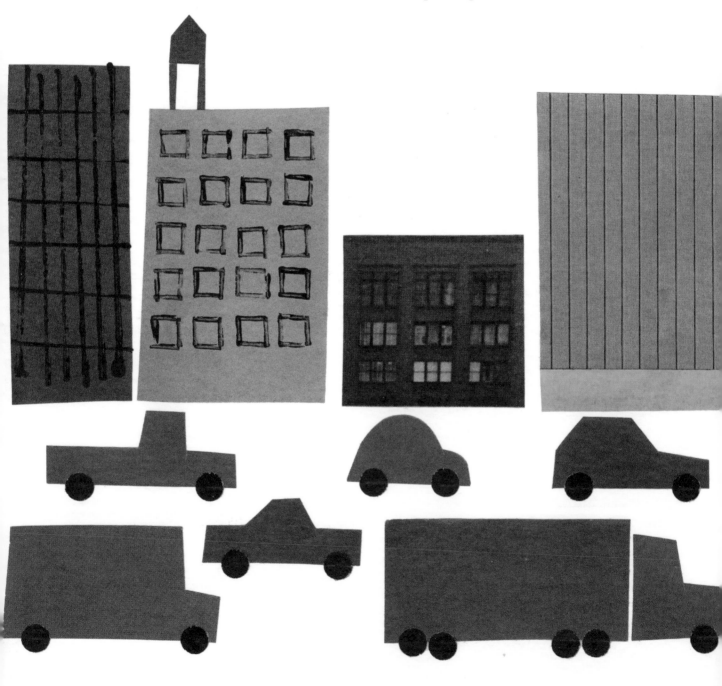

and here's a wing
from a butterfly

here's a cherry if you need a snack

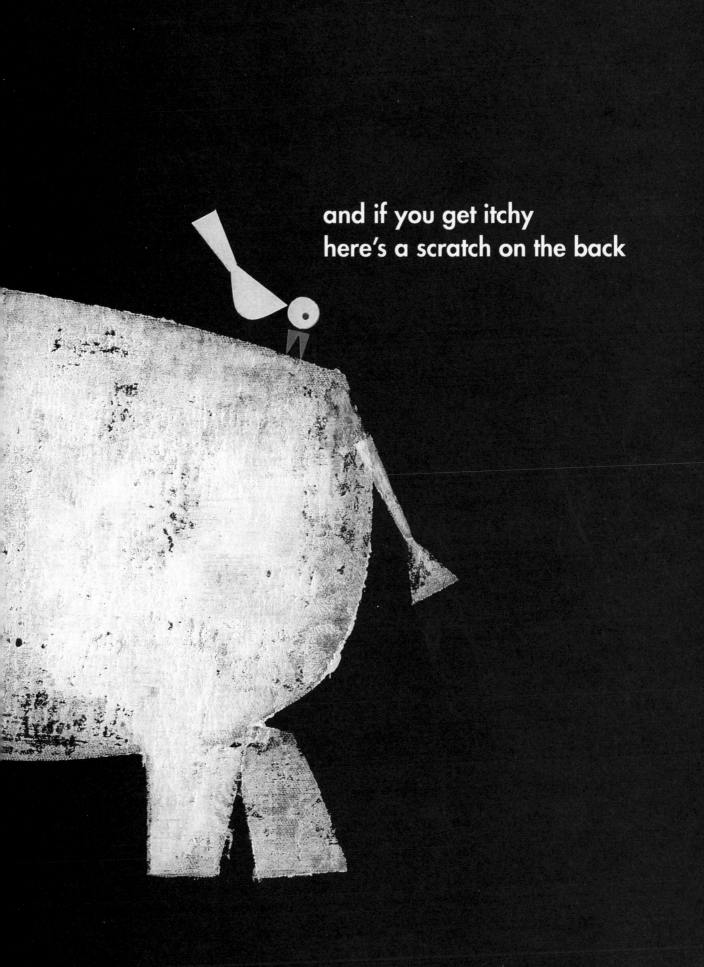

and if you get itchy
here's a scratch on the back

here's a rock to skip

and a coin to wish

and a fork

and a spoon

and a cup

and a dish

and just in case you want to sing
here's a la la la

and a

ding
ding
ding

here's a joke
if you want to laugh

bye, son!

and here's your
toothbrush

**and your
favourite
giraffe**

here's a blanket

and here's a dream

and some kisses
on your head

here's a pillow

and here's a song
for when you go to bed

and just in case you want to cry
here is a tissue
and here's a sigh

here's an umbrella
in case it rains

and some honey for your tea

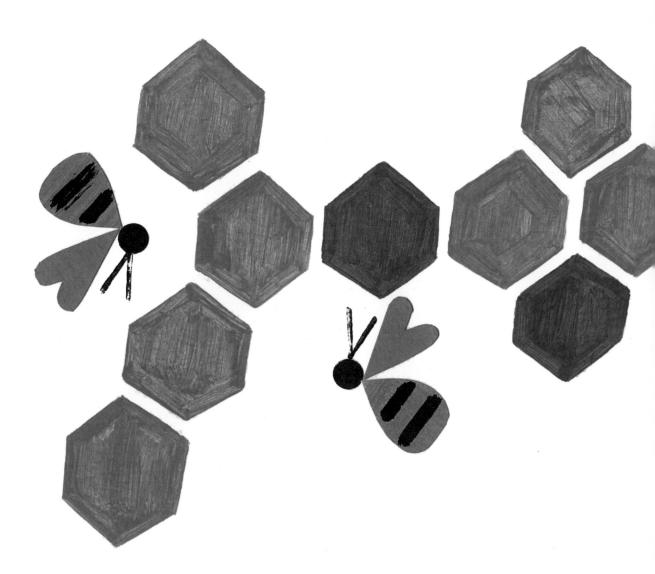

and here is a map
with an x on the spot
to find your way
home to me